Water for One,
Water for Everyone

To Jennifer, a brand-new elementary school teacher
and our family's first.   S.S.

To Mo, with love.   M.L.

Published by The Millbrook Press, Inc.
2 Old New Milford Road
Brookfield, CT 06804

Printed in the United States of America
5   4   3   2   1

Library of Congress Cataloging-in-Publication Data
Swinburne, Stephen R.
Water for one, water for everyone : a counting
book of African animals / by Stephen R. Swinburne;
illustrated by Melinda Levine.
p.   cm.
Summary: A counting tale in which native animals,
from one tortoise to ten elephants, arrive at a
Kenyan waterhole.
ISBN 0-7613-0269-7 (lib. bdg.)
ISBN 0-7613-0347-2 (pbk.)
[1. Zoology—Africa—Fiction. 2. Animals—
Fiction. 3. Counting.] I. Levine, Melinda, ill.
II. Title.
PZ7.S98135Wat   1998
[E]—dc21   97-14429   CIP AC

WATER
for One,
WATER
for Everyone

A Counting Book of African Animals

BY STEPHEN R. SWINBURNE

ILLUSTRATED BY MELINDA LEVINE

The Millbrook Press   Brookfield, Connecticut

On a very dry day in Africa, one tortoise found a lonely waterhole.

The tortoise tasted the water and the water in the hole went down.

Two bee-eaters
flew over and settled
beside the tortoise
to take a drink.

The bee-eaters sipped
and sipped and the water
in the hole went down.

Three baboons shuffled past and paused to drink.

The baboons slurped and slurped and the water in the hole went down.

Four warthogs rooted nearby and stopped for a drink.

The warthogs guzzled and guzzled and the water in the hole went down.

Five ostriches pranced by and bent way over to drink.

The ostriches swallowed and swallowed and the water in the hole went down.

Six gazelles bounced over and joined the others.

The gazelles gulped and gulped and the water in the hole went down.

Seven wildebeests galloped close by and stopped to take a sip.

The wildebeests lapped and lapped and the water in the hole went down.

Eight zebras browsed nearby and came with a mighty thirst.

The zebras drank and drank and the water in the hole went down.

Nine impalas arrived
thirsty and dry.

The impalas swigged and
swigged and the water in
the hole went down.

Ten elephants thundered in and stuck ten long trunks in the waterhole.

The elephants snorted
and sucked and the
water in the hole…

disappeared!

The tortoise sighed.

The ostriches shuffled.

The bee-eaters cackled.

The baboons scratched.

The warthogs grunted.

The gazelles bleated.

The wildebeests stamped.

The zebras neighed.

The impalas snorted.

The elephants hung their heads.

Then they swung their trunks to the sky and trumpeted with all their might to some passing clouds.

The clouds cracked and filled the hole with rain.

And then there was water
for everyone.

Author's Note

The waterhole in the story is in Kenya in east-central Africa. Many of the same animals are found in other African countries such as Tanzania, Uganda, and Sudan. Swahili is the language spoken in many east-central African countries.

COUNTING TO TEN IN SWAHILI

One	Moja	Six	Sita
Two	Mbili	Seven	Saba
Three	Tatu	Eight	Nane
Four	Nne	Nine	Tisa
Five	Tano	Ten	Kumi

AFRICAN ANIMALS IN SWAHILI

Tortoise	Kobe
Bee-eater	Nyengere
Baboon	Nyani
Warthog	Ngiri
Ostrich	Mbuni
Gazelle	Swara
Wildebeest	Nyumbu mwitu
Zebra	Punda milia
Impala	Paa
Elephant	Ndovu